ORCA
YOUNG
READERS

Catching Spring

Sylvia Olsen

D0107063

ORCA BOOK PUBLISHERS

National Library of Canada Cataloguing in Publication Data

Olsen, Sylvia, 1955-
Catching spring / Sylvia Olsen.

"Orca young reader".
ISBN 1-55143-298-6

I. Title.

PS8579.L728C38 2004   jC813'.6   C2004-901633-4

Library of Congress Control Number: 2004103565

Summary: In 1957, Bobby, a First Nations boy, longs to enter a fishing derby, but he has no boat, no money and he has to work on the day of the derby.

Free teachers' guide available.

Orca Book Publishers gratefully acknowledges the support for its publishing programs provided by the following agencies: the Government of Canada through the Book Publishing Industry Development Program (BPIDP), the Canada Council for the Arts, and the British Columbia Arts Council.

Cover design by Lynn O'Rourke
Cover & interior illustrations by Darlene Gait

In Canada:	**In the United States:**
Orca Book Publishers	Orca Book Publishers
1030 North Park Street	PO Box 468
Victoria, BC Canada	Custer, WA USA
V8T 1C6	98240-0468

07 06 05 04 • 6 5 4 3 2 1

Printed and bound in Canada
Printed on 100% post-consumer recycled paper,
100% old growth forest free, processed chlorine free
using vegetable, low VOC inks.

1

Bobby flew through the kitchen and grabbed his jacket and an extra pair of socks from the freshly folded pile of laundry on the kitchen table. He stuffed the socks into his pocket and picked up an apple from a wooden box on the floor.

Mom appeared at the front door. "Not so fast, young man," she said, pulling him toward her and kissing him on the cheek. "You be careful down there, Bobby. I worry about you."

"You don't have nothing to worry about, Mom." Bobby paused to give her an extra hug. "Dan takes care of me."

Mom spat on her fingers and patted Bobby's hair down. "Here, take another apple and put it in your pocket." She pulled a rosy red apple out of her apron pocket.

There wasn't much room. His pockets were full of thick socks, but Bobby managed to tuck the apple in safely.

He looked at the battery clock hanging on the wall next to the woodstove. Twenty-five minutes after four o'clock.

"Thanks, Mom. I gotta go. I don't wanna be late," he shouted over his shoulder. Mom had brought the big round clock home from the church basement sale a few weeks earlier. The bold black numbers were easy to read, but the smiling, blond man and woman in the picture stamped in the center of the clock didn't look anything like Bobby's mom and dad.

When Bobby first learned how to tell time the year before in Sister Madeleine's grade three class, he sometimes had trouble with the big hand and the little hand. But now that his family had a clock of their own, Bobby kept track of what time he got out of bed, what time Mom started the laundry on Mondays, what time the green pickup truck came by on Wednesdays selling vegetables and other stuff like that.

Now Bobby had a job. When Dan said, "I'll see you at five o'clock," Bobby made sure that he left the house before half-past-four to give himself time to run down to the dock and get there early.

Lucky and Ezra were huddled in front of the house. "Hey, Bro," Ezra called out as Bobby jumped around them, "want to play marbles?"

"I'd love to, but I gotta go," Bobby replied, "or I'll be late for work."

Bobby's brothers were hunched on either side of the smooth hollow Bobby had helped to carve out of the hard-packed dirt next to the steps.

"I'll let you have my cat's eye. The small one I won from Soupy yesterday." Ezra held the shiny marble out to his older brother. "Pretty nice, don't you think? I'll let you have it if you play for a while."

Bobby watched the gold and orange and blue and green as he rolled the glass sphere around in the palm of his hand. It was beautiful. He couldn't believe Ezra was willing to give it to him. That would make twelve small and four big cat's eyes if he would just stay and play marbles with his brothers.

He hesitated. Maybe he could play for ten minutes. Then he would run extra hard and make it to Dan's marina just in time. He thought for a moment more and passed the marble back.

"Thanks anyway, Bro. But I gotta get to work. Dan's gonna be waiting for me. And it's past twenty-five minutes after four o'clock."

Time didn't mean anything to Ezra and Lucky. Ezra was going into grade three this year and Lucky was only going into grade one. Neither one of his younger brothers paid much attention to the time, and Bobby didn't think they ever would. They were more interested in playing marbles or skittle ball or climbing the oak tree and hanging upside down by their knees until their faces turned purple and their eyes bugged out.

It's not that Bobby didn't like to play with his brothers, especially marbles. It was just that since the summer and since he met Dan Adams, he had a job. Every Saturday morning Bobby worked at the marina, sweeping the dock, hosing it down, cleaning the boats and sometimes even gutting fish and selling tackle. Once in a while, like tonight, Bobby slept overnight in Dan's big fish boat that was winched up on the ways for repairs. That's why Bobby needed the extra socks to keep his feet warm.

Tomorrow morning Bobby would be ready first thing for the fishermen who arrived before the sun was up. Bobby's favorite thing in the whole world was fishing, so he didn't mind leaving the cat's eye behind, although he would have loved to watch the sun splash on the colored glass as the marble turned.

Bobby was the Tsartlip Indian Reserve marble champion. His younger brother and Soupy from next door could flick the marbles hard, maybe harder than Bobby, but they weren't accurate and they didn't pay attention to the other marbles in the game. Even Bobby's older brothers couldn't beat him.

Only Cousin Glass Eyes could play marbles as well as Bobby. Bobby couldn't understand how he did it with his eyes all shrunk down behind his thick glasses. Long after all the other boys had lost interest and found something else to do, Glass Eyes and Bobby would continue until the last marble was traded. Glass Eyes knew how to take his time and stay focused. But if you wanted to know who the Tsartlip village marble champion was, you could ask pretty well any of the boys on the reserve and they would tell you the same thing: Bobby. Even Glass Eyes might tell you that.

"Hey," Bobby said to his brothers as he turned down the path, "I'll be home at lunch tomorrow. I'll play with you then. Save that marble!"

"Yeah, okay," Ezra said. He didn't like it now his brother had a job. Nothing could keep Bobby away from the fishing dock. Not even a cat's eye marble.

Bobby sped down the path. The hot afternoon sun sparkled on the flat waters of Indian Bay. The hills would soon block the golden light, and the autumn evening chill would settle in. The path wound through the oak grove and around by Grandpa Abe's place, or at least where he used to live before they took him to the hospital. Just past Grandpa's old smokehouse, Bobby had to jump over the stream that was not much more than a trickle since the summer had been so hot. The path widened through the field past the Jones's and Samuels's places until it met the road. When Bobby's feet hit the pavement, he turned right and rushed past the craft store and the milkshake shop and toward the stairs under the big red sign that said DAN ADAMS'S MARINA. He stopped and waved when he saw Dan.

Kids' Fishing Derby

August 30, 1957 Dan Adams's Marina

BOYS AND GIRLS AGES 8-13

FIRST PRIZE (NEW BIKE)

SECOND PRIZE: Fishing Rod, Tackle and Tackle Box.

DERBY RULES:

1. Kids must set their own bait
2. hold their own pole
3. reel in the fish
4. net the fish
5. kill the fish
All fish must be weighed by 1 pm

BY AUGUST 30

$5 registration fee

2

"Bobby, come on down," Dan hollered. "Come over here and give me a hand."

Bobby skipped down the stairs. Bright yellow posters hung on the posts on either side of the dock. Dan handed him a stack of the yellow papers. Bobby read the top one carefully. He traced his finger over every word.

Kids' Fishing Derby

August 30, 1957   Dan Adams's Marina

Boys and Girls Ages 8–13

FIRST PRIZE: NEW BIKE

SECOND PRIZE: Fishing rod, tackle and tackle box

DERBY RULES:
1. Kids must set their own bait
2. hold their own pole
3. reel in the fish
4. net the fish
5. kill the fish
All fish must be weighed by 1 pm

$5.00 registration fee

It was the picture of the bike that really caught Bobby's attention. He couldn't tell for sure because the picture was kind of fuzzy, but the bike looked shiny and new. It had a rattrap bolted to the back and a light attached to the front. When Bobby looked closely he could see whitewall tires. At least he thought he could.

"You want to see the bike?" Dan asked. "We got it here."

"Really? Yeah, I wanna see it!"

"Come on then. It's in the tackle shop." Dan strode into the small shed and Bobby followed. Behind the high glass display case filled with lures, weights, flashers and other fishing tackle, strung up from the ceiling by thick ropes, was the most beautiful bike Bobby had ever seen. It was blue with chrome fenders, and when the sun through the door glistened off the wheels, it looked like it had a million spokes. Bobby figured it might be a little big for him. He might have trouble keeping both his feet on the pedals at the same time, but in no time he would grow into it.

Bobby had an old bike once. Mom had pushed it home with one hand while she packed her groceries with the other all the way from the Bay Mercantile. She said Mrs. Miller, the woman at the store, had given it to her—for nothing—and that one of the kids might want it. Long before she got the bike home, Mom found out that the wheel was bent. No kid would be able to ride it. But rather than leave it on the side of the road like garbage, she pushed it home. Mom always figured that if something was free, someone should be able to make something of it. Bobby agreed, so he hit the bent and rusty front wheel with a rock over and over again until it was straight and turned without the tire rubbing on the frame. Bobby rode that bike for months until the tire finally burst.

Bobby's jaw hung loose as he gaped at the brand-new bike. It was beautiful. Really beautiful.

Finally he said, "Some kid is sure gonna be lucky when he wins that." He wanted to reach up and rub his hand along the shiny posts and turn the wheels and watch the spokes whirl.

But "Come on, Bobby, my boy," Dan said. "We gotta get these posters up so everyone knows we're having a derby. We want to get all the kids we can to sign up."

Bobby passed him a paper and Dan stapled it to a post. By the time they were finished, yellow signs hung everywhere as if a festival or a circus or a party was being planned.

"I'll take the rest of the posters up to town later and staple them to telephone poles at the Bay Mercantile, the gas station and the post office," Dan said. He tucked the posters under the counter in the tackle shop. Bobby stared at the poster stuck to the door. He read it again.

He was ten years old, the right age. He stood a pretty good chance of winning the bike if only he could find a way to enter the derby. He knew how to set the bait and pull the fish in. He even knew how to hold the net and scoop the fish out of the water. Bobby looked at the poster again. Five dollars. That was the hard part. How was he going to get five dollars? He made one dollar each weekend from Dan. He gave his mom half of that, which left him with fifty cents. With three weeks until the derby he could only save $1.50. Then Bobby thought of something else. Even if some miracle happened and he found the money, he didn't have anyone to rent a boat for him.

And what about Dan? Who would help Dan on the day of the derby? Who would help the fishermen with their boats, and who would help them when they came back? That was Bobby's job. The whole thing was just too much trouble; maybe he should stop thinking about going in the derby. And winning the bike.

Bobby lingered at the door of the tackle shop so he could take one more long look at the bike before he started his work. He couldn't quite see what the seat was like, but it looked like black leather because of how it glistened in the light. It looked soft and comfortable.

He could get to work in no time if he rode the blue bike. He would never be late. He would have to lock it up to a post, as he had seen some fishermen do when they got to the dock. He could chain the bike to the post right beside the boat where he slept. That way he could catch a glimpse of it during the night. Just to make sure it was all right.

Dan walked back into the tackle shop with a big black book and a metal box.

"This is the registration book," he said, thumping the heavy book onto the counter. "We'll get everyone to put their name, address and phone number in here." Dan pulled a little gold key from his pocket and opened the box. "We'll put the registration money in this box."

Bobby didn't know if Dan was talking to him or to himself.

"I'm gonna put the key in the cash register," Dan continued. He slid the box carefully into a cupboard under the counter. "You wait until tomorrow, young man. We'll be swamped with people wanting to sign up." Dan slapped his hands together the way he did when he had finished something. He turned and looked at Bobby. "Okay, Bobby, my boy. It's time to get to work. I want you to pack the boxes of tackle and set them in the shop and hose off the dock and check the boats to make sure they're ready for tomorrow. They've all gotta be cleaned out and ready to go except numbers 18 and 22."

3

Bobby did just what Dan said. The boxes of tackle were heavy. Bobby stacked them off to the side of the shop, where Dan wouldn't trip over them in the morning. He straightened the stacks into neat piles. Bobby liked his work to be just right. He liked edges to be straight and things to be in order, one thing after the other.

After Bobby moved the tackle, he turned on the water and dragged the hose to the far end of the dock where it stuck right out into the bay. He squished his finger over the end of the hose to create water pressure and waved the hose slowly back and forth across the heavy planks, making sure the wood was slick and clean. Sometimes he had to press hard and hold the hose in one spot for a while to loosen up the dry fish guts or bird poop that stuck tight to the dock.

When he was finished cleaning he headed down the dock to check out the boats. Dan had told him to make sure all the boats were tied up with secure knots. Each boat needed two life jackets, one paddle, a club and a wooden fish box under the bench. And Bobby had to make sure there was no garbage left in the boats. No gum wrappers or banana peels or wax paper stuck in the corners. Dan had said he would teach Bobby to gas up the boats after he had worked a little longer. For now he was just supposed to check the gear and the knots and the garbage.

Twenty-three boats lined the dock, not counting Dan's own boat, which was different from the ones he rented out. Then there was the old shabby boat that was tied up at the very end of the dock and got in the way. The rental boats were big enough for four grown men plus all the stuff they loaded in when they went fishing and a kid, if he was small. A short wooden canopy covered the steering wheel so that two of the men could sit inside and two had to sit outside. The boats were wooden. Dan called them clinkers. Bobby didn't know what that word meant, but he liked the sound of it.

Nine boats were tied to one side of the dock and fourteen were tied to the other. When Bobby climbed out of one boat and into the next, they jostled and tipped and clunked against the dock. Each boat was painted blue on the bottom and white on top, except for Number 1. It was chipped and peeled red on the bottom and black on top.

On the front of each boat was painted a number and a name. The boats were called *Chinook, Coho, Abalone, Mussel, Sea Urchin, Octopus* and names like that. All stuff from the sea, Dan said. Stuff you could eat. Bobby smiled when he climbed into *Shrimp*. It should be smaller than the other boats, but it was just the same size. By the time Bobby finished checking the gear, the sun had disappeared behind the mountains and it was getting pretty chilly.

"I'm finished," Bobby said to Dan, who was sitting on a lawn chair in front of the tackle shop. "They're all decked out and ready to go."

"Attaboy," Dan said. "Now you better hit the sack. You gotta wake up before the sun."

"Okay," Bobby said. "Anything else you want done?"

"Nope, you got it," Dan replied. "I left you something to eat on the boat."

"Thanks," Bobby said. "Good night. Don't forget to wake me up."

"Don't worry about that."

Bobby slept in Dan's boat, which was pulled out of the water and sat up on braces, ready to be painted. When Dan had time he scraped the old green paint off the boat and sanded the trim. But for now the boat was Bobby's house. He climbed up the ladder and into the cabin, where a plate of sandwiches and a glass of milk waited beside the cot that Dan had set up in the small room.

Bobby shivered as he pulled the apple out of his pocket and set it next to the plate. He pulled out the socks and put them on his feet. He took off his coat, jumped into the sleeping bag and laid his coat over his feet. He took his time eating half the peanut butter-and-jam sandwich and drinking half the glass of milk. He left the other half on the plate for the next morning. It was getting dark out so Bobby could barely find the clean dishcloth Dan had left in the cabin. He shook it out and placed it over his food.

Bobby lay down and pulled the sleeping bag up to his nose. He listened to the water lapping at the boats as they gently rubbed together. He breathed in the salt air and thought how much he loved the dock. It didn't only smell like salt water; it also smelled like fish. No matter whether there were fish around or not, everything was fishy, just the way Bobby liked it.

When Bobby closed his eyes, it was only a minute before he was dreaming of riding a bike. Not an old rusty bike with a bent tire, but a bright bold blue bike with fenders so shiny that he could see his face in them. He rode the bike up the road, through town, back down the lane past the farms and then home to the reserve. In his dream he leaned the bike up against the front porch while he played marbles with Glass Eyes and won another big cat's eye.

4

Squawk, squawk, squawk.

Bobby popped his head out of his sleeping bag and opened one eye. It was still completely dark. The end of his nose was cold. Seagulls scratched and squawked on the roof of the boat cabin just above his head. Bobby lay still for a minute. His favorite things about sleeping on the boat were the sounds and smells. He wished he could stay in bed and listen to the water and the birds and the seals. But *Clump Clump Clump.* Dan's feet came stomping down the stairs. Dan's house hung over the end of the dock, right on the beach.

"Get up, sleepy," Dan hollered. "If you don't get up soon you'll grow roots in that sleeping bag."

It must be four-thirty in the morning or five at the latest, Bobby thought. If he saved his money, one day he would be able to buy himself a watch. He would wear it every day. Then he would know what time it got light in the morning and what time the fishermen packed up their rods. He would know, when they said the fish were biting at six-thirty, exactly what time that was. If he had a watch of his own, Bobby would know what time the first fisherman arrived on the dock and what time Dan stomped down the stairs.

Bobby sat up and chomped down the last half of his peanut butter-and-jam sandwich and gulped the rest of his glass of milk, which was still cold. It was only August, but it almost felt like autumn. He swung his legs over the side of the bed and dipped his feet right into his black boots. Bobby knew that fishermen want to be out in their boats when the first light of morning breaks on the water. That's when the fish are hungry and biting. So Bobby rushed out the cabin door and down the ladder. He stuffed the apple his mother gave him back in his pocket for later.

"I'm coming," he called out to Dan wherever he was.

Bobby ran up the dock when he saw the light in the tackle shop.

"Good morning there, boy," Dan exclaimed.

"Morning."

"How did you sleep in that there boat? Did you get seasick?" Dan always laughed before and after he said something, so it was hard for Bobby to know if he was joking or saying something important. Bobby almost began to explain to Dan that the boat wasn't even in the water, when he remembered that Dan probably already knew that.

"Got woke up by the seagulls," Bobby said.

"Those gall-darn birds probably wanted your sandwich." Dan laughed again.

"All the boats are full this morning. Two calls came in already so we don't have a single boat to spare."

"Want me to go down and check Number 18 and Number 22?" Bobby asked, proud that he knew which boats hadn't been checked the night before.

"Sure." Dan laughed again. "I didn't gas them up either, so can you haul the gas can down and fill them up for me?"

Did Dan forget that Bobby hadn't ever gassed up the boats before? Bobby ran out the door figuring out how he would get the job done. After all, he had watched Dan do it enough times.

"Make sure to wipe down the seats and steering wheel," Dan called down the dock.

By the time Bobby had unscrewed the gas cap on Number 18, the sky was dark gray instead of black. He made sure that not one drop of gas escaped and ran down the side of the tank. He screwed the cap back on tight and wiped and checked the tackle in both boats before he lugged the gas can back up the dock.

Fishermen were already gathered at the tackle shop. Some were buying last-minute lures and bait while others were reading the poster and signing their sons and nephews and younger brothers up for the derby.

"You gonna catch the biggest fish?" a man wearing a bright red toque asked as Bobby led him to Number 12, *Tuna*. "I bet there isn't much you don't know about fishing this inlet. Your people have been around here for a long time."

Bobby hadn't thought much about it, but the man was right. His father and grand-father and every grandfather before that lived in Tsartlip, right on the Saanich Inlet. They were Tsartlip people and had always lived in the same spot. They had been fishing out of the bay since forever. Maybe that was why he was just as happy sitting in a canoe out in the middle of the bay as he was standing on the beach. Both places were home to him.

The man was big and round. He wore a red checkered shirt and his baggy black trousers were held up with wide yellow suspenders strapped over his belly and chest. His rubber boots were so big that Bobby thought he could almost crawl right into one of them and disappear.

"I'm not going to fish in the derby," Bobby said. "I don't have five dollars, and I have to help Dan out with the kids and boats and tackle and stuff."

"You tell that Dan from me that I think he oughta let a boy like you fish that derby. You don't want to be sitting here while all the other kids head out." The man pointed his finger right down Bobby's throat as if he were scolding him for something.

Bobby didn't tell Dan what the man said, but he wished the man would tell Dan himself. Not that it would do much good. Even if Dan did give him the time off, he still didn't have five dollars or a boat.

That morning Bobby worked nonstop packing tackle boxes, blankets, thermoses, fishing rods and a lot of other things like books and gloves and boots and radios and extra coats and cushions. He didn't know why people needed stuff like that while they were fishing. It just got in the way.

After the last fisherman revved up his engine and puffed a cloud of blue smoke into the air, Bobby sat on the end of the dock and watched the boat get smaller and smaller until it finally disappeared around the point. He pulled the apple out of his pocket and chewed eagerly on the crisp juicy fruit.

"That was one busy morning," Dan said when he sat down next to Bobby. "Feels good to get them all out. I wonder what they'll be catching. I hear it's pretty good out at Bamberton." He pointed across the inlet. "They're catching a lot of spring early on and then late in the afternoon too."

Bobby thought about the stories his grandpa had told him about paddling a canoe out into the bay. He said you could see so many fish that you could have reached down and picked them out of the water by their tails if they weren't so slippery. Bobby wasn't sure the story was true, especially when his grandpa told him that he scooped the fish out of the water with the net, no fishing line at all. Just dip the net over the side of the canoe and pull it up, Grandpa said. And then he said that one day he dumped so many fish in the canoe that it almost sank!

Bobby wished his grandpa hadn't got sick and hadn't been taken up to Nanaimo to the Indian hospital. If his grandpa was still around, he would have found the five dollars and entered Bobby in the derby. He would have paddled his old canoe while Bobby held onto the fishing rod. And he would have known exactly where to find the biggest fish of all.

5

"You gonna stick around until the boats get back?" Dan asked.

"Sure."

"Then you head up and get yourself a pop from the tackle shop. You must be thirsty." Dan slapped Bobby's back so hard the last bite of his apple almost got stuck in his throat.

Bobby wished his dad was there to see him work at the fish dock, but his dad wasn't around much. Not anymore. Whenever Dad was at home he didn't have much time for Bobby, not with all the other kids in the family and with Mom needing him to fix the stuff that got broken since the last time he was home. Bobby didn't know where his dad went between visits, and he didn't like to ask. It wasn't something Mom said much about. Once in a while Dad brought money home, and Mom was happy for a few days and really sad when he left, but most of the time when Dad got home he wanted to borrow money from Mom. After those visits Mom was just as happy to see him go.

Bobby helped Mom out as much as he could with the money. Every Saturday when Dan gave him a dollar, he gave Mom fifty cents. The previous weekend he gave her the whole dollar because money was getting pretty tight around the house. In the summer, when Bobby's family picked strawberries or raspberries, Bobby gave all his earnings to Mom. So did the rest of the kids, and there were ten of them. That way she could buy hamburger or even hot dogs, which were Bobby's favorite.

Other than that, the only money Mom had coming in was what she earned knitting sweaters. Every weekend she traveled to Victoria and sold her sweaters. Bobby and the girls learned how to knit too. They helped Mom out making hats and socks, especially in the winter. Mom sold the things the kids knit. And with all the money put together, Mom made sure everyone had a good meal in their stomachs and clothes on their backs. No one starved or froze to death, although sometimes Bobby's stomach was still growling even after supper. So Bobby worked hard. He wanted to make sure the younger kids didn't have that hungry feeling, at least not very often.

Bobby threw his apple core into the water and watched it float away. Then he ran up the dock to the tackle shop. Usually, if anyone treated him to pop, he had to share it with Ezra and Lucky or with Lacy and Pudding, his older sisters. He usually got more when he shared with the boys. The girls were bigger and they never let him get more than a sip or two.

He opened the cooler and rummaged through the bottles for a root beer—the best kind of pop. He took off the cap with the opener nailed to the end of the counter, then licked the moist bottle top. The tingle of root beer made his eyes water.

Bobby swaggered out of the tackle shop, pop in hand. At that moment the world was just as it should be: a good night's sleep on the boat, a hard morning's work and a bottle of pop—all to yourself. If he could think of a way to enter the fishing derby, his life would be perfect.

Dan picked up the derby registration book and sat on his lawn chair as Bobby sucked on his root beer.

"We've got nine entrants already," Dan said. "And no one even knew about the derby this morning." He ran his finger down the list and grinned. "We're gonna be busier than a dog in flea season."

Just after midmorning, the boats started coming back and tying up. Everyone had caught something, and a few of the fish boxes were filled to the brim. Bobby pulled cohos, springs and even a sockeye or two up onto the counter and helped the fishermen gut and clean their catch. He tossed the guts and fish eggs twoard the water. Seagulls swooped down and caught the entrails in midair and swallowed them without so much as a gulp. The fish guts must sit like a lump in their stomachs, Bobby thought.

The sun was high in the sky when Dan sauntered down to the cleaning bench.

"You must be dead beat, Bobby. Why don't you clean up and head on home? I can take over from here." He pushed a dollar bill into Bobby's hand. "You've been a big help this morning. See you next Friday."

Bobby wiped his hand and then wiped the blood off the dollar and stuffed it into his pocket. As he turned to head home he saw the big man with the yellow suspenders tying up his boat. Bobby didn't know why, but he liked that man. He ran down the dock and asked if he could help him pack his stuff up the dock.

"You bet you can, young man," the man said.

Bobby hung the man's bag over his shoulder and packed his thermos and tackle box.

"I got two coho and three springs," the man said proudly. "And they're so big I can barely carry them."

The fish must be really big. The man looked strong enough to carry just about anything. And a big man like that wouldn't be in the habit of admitting that something was too heavy for him.

"Well, young man, are you heading home?" he asked. His voice was as big as his belly.

"Yeah. Pretty soon."

The man reached into his pocket and pulled out a dollar bill. He held it up in the air and said loudly, "This should help you get the registration money if that Dan Adams would let you off work for the derby."

Bobby looked around quickly to see if Dan heard what the man said. But Dan was talking to someone up by the tackle shop. If he heard anything at all, it was probably only a word or two.

"Thank you very much," Bobby said politely. "I wish I could enter the derby, but I doubt I can."

Inside, Bobby knew for sure. He knew he wasn't going to be able to enter the derby even if he did get enough money. But he didn't want to tell that to the man in the yellow suspenders. Not after he gave him a whole dollar.

On the way home, Bobby didn't run as fast as he did the night before. He was tired, and in a certain way he wished Dan Adams wasn't having a fishing derby and that he didn't have to miss it. Bobby decided it wasn't worth saving his money for the derby. Even if he did make the money, he should give it to Mom. She needed it more than he did.

Ezra and Lucky weren't outside playing marbles when Bobby reached the front stairs. The yard was deserted. That was unusual. He let himself in the front door and found Mom sitting on her chair knitting a sweater.

"How was work, Bobby?" she asked.

"Okay."

"Come here and let me take a look at you," she said. "You don't sound so good."

"I'm just tired," Bobby said as he plopped himself onto the bed next to his mom. "I made two dollars. One from Dan. Then a guy with yellow suspenders gave me a whole dollar."

Bobby fished around in his pocket and yanked out the two bills.

"Here." He tossed the money onto his mother's lap.

"You keep one, Bobby," she said. "You don't have to give me all your money."

"Naw," Bobby said. "It's all right. What do I have to spend it on anyway?"

"What's wrong, son?" Mom asked.

"Nothing." Bobby wasn't about to tell her about the fishing derby.

He flopped back on the bed. "I'm just going to lie down for a while."

6

When Bobby woke up, sweat was dripping down his forehead and Mom was no longer sitting on her chair next to his bed. He pulled himself up, still feeling groggy and heavy headed. Voices were coming from out in front of the house. And Mom was clanging pots and pans in the kitchen. Bobby slipped off the bed and dragged himself to the front door to see what was going on.

"Hey, Bro, you're home!" Ezra yelled.

"Come on, Bobby," Soupy called out. "Everyone's coming over for a tournament. Teams against teams."

Ezra and Soupy had their marbles lined up in shallow grooves cleared out in the soft dirt. They had their cat's eyes at one end and then the plain marbles separated by colors, the black ones with the black ones and the yellow ones with the yellow ones and the green ones with the green ones. Like that.

"Bobby's on my team," Lucky blurted out. He held his marbles tightly in his hands.

"No way, Lucky," Ezra argued. "We haven't picked teams yet. You have to wait till everyone gets here. And who said you get on a team anyway?"

Lucky didn't always get to play marbles with the boys. Usually Ezra would play with him only when there was just the two of them. Lucky only had three marbles of his own, and none of them were cat's eyes. Just a few weeks earlier he'd had five or six, but he had lost them under the bed or in the long grass outside like he always did. Or the other boys won them. When Lucky did get to play he would lose all his marbles right away, but not before he knocked the other boys' marbles all over the place. That was the part Bobby didn't like very much. He hated it when he was just about to take a shot and Lucky leaned in close to watch, bumped the marbles and messed the whole thing up.

Sometimes Bobby felt kind of bad for Lucky. He wished his little brother had a few more marbles. He wished Lucky would learn how to play properly so everyone didn't always want to get rid of him. Bobby wished he had kept at least ten cents of his money from Dan to buy Lucky some marbles.

"Hold on, guys," Bobby said as he turned back toward the door. "I'll get my marbles."

Bobby ran to the bed that he shared with Ezra and Lucky. Their bedroom was the living room where Mom knit and the other kids sat around and played cards and Monopoly. Bobby pushed a pile of wool aside, knelt and reached far underneath the bed. He pulled out an old shoebox and took off the lid. His leather gloves were on top, the ones his grandpa had given him before he got taken to hospital. They were old and curled up at the fingertips, but Bobby was going to keep them safe until they fit right. Once in a while Bobby opened the box just to push his hands into the gloves. They felt smooth and soft. He could feel where his grandpa's fingers had been. Sometimes when he pulled the gloves off he stuck them up to his nose and breathed in deep and remembered the smell of his grandpa.

This time Bobby set the gloves aside and lifted out the dark blue cloth bag tied around the top with a gold twisted string. He set the gloves neatly back in the box on top of his pens and pencils for school, his pink eraser that was almost all used up but not quite, the American silver dollar that Uncle Howard had given him and the key chain he had found on the side of the road and was saving for when he got a car of his own. Bobby put the lid back on and pushed the box deep under his bed where no one could even see a corner of it if they looked.

When he got back outside, Speedy, Joey, Flipper and Dodgey had joined the other boys.

"Are we waiting for Glass Eyes?" Flipper asked. Some of the boys had proper names, like Bobby and Joey, but if you had ears as big as Flipper's there wasn't a chance anyone was going to call you Albert. Or Glass Eyes. Who was gonna call him Emmanuel? Not with his glasses as thick as a book.

In Tsartlip, people liked to think of nicknames. And once you got a nickname you were stuck with it, sometimes for the rest of your life. That's what happened to the old man who lived down a ways and across the field from Bobby's house—his name was Scoop. When Bobby asked Mom how the old man got a name like Scoop, Mom said that he had been called Scoop for so long that most people forgot his real name.

"Let's wait for Glass Eyes," Joey said. "Then we'll pick teams."

"I'm on Bobby's team," Lucky said again.

He didn't seem to care that Ezra didn't want him to play.

The boys tossed marbles until they heard Glass Eyes running down the path toward the house.

"Hey, man, hurry up," Ezra called.

"I'm coming, I'm coming," he shouted. "Don't start without me."

When Glass Eyes joined the group, everyone started to talk at once.

"I'm on Bobby's team."

"No, you're not."

"I want to be on Glass Eyes's team."

"I'm not playing if I have to be on Lucky's team again. He wrecks everything."

"Shut up. You'll be on whatever team picks you."

"Who're the captains?"

"Bobby. Glass Eyes."

"No way. They're always the captains."

"Okay, then you be a captain."

"Okay. I'm one of the captians," Joey shouted. "Who wants to be the other one?" His voice sounded like he was in charge, so everyone listened.

"Me," Ezra piped up.

That seemed to be all right with everyone, so Ezra and Joey stood one on one side of the hole and one on the other. The rest of the boys shuffled into a group in front of the captains.

Joey threw his hand in the air. "I'm picking first."

"No way," Ezra said.

"I was the first captain," Joey argued back.

Ezra must have seen some sense in Joey's argument because he leaned back on his heels and waited.

Joey pointed. "Bobby."

Ezra was quick to pick next. "Glass Eyes."

"Speedy," Joey said.

"Soupy."

"Flipper."

"Dodgey."

That left Lucky standing across from the boys all by himself. He looked at the two teams.

"We both have four. It's even steven, so Lucky can't play," Ezra said.

When Lucky burst out crying, the other boys all said at the same time, "He can be on your team."

Finally Bobby said, "He's on my team." He looked at his little brother. "Wipe your nose and quit crying. I'll give you another marble if you promise to stay out of the way."

Lucky brightened up instantly. He dug around eagerly in Bobby's marble bag.

"Not a cat's eye," Bobby said.

"I want a green one," Lucky said gleefully. "A bright green one like this." He held a lime green marble between his chubby, grubby fingers.

"Fine," Bobbie nodded. "It's yours."

7

The boys circled the hole. Four on one
side and five on the other. Bobby cleared
the way so Lucky could take a few shots.
Then he pushed Lucky back to make sure
he didn't wreck the game for everyone
else.

Each boy took his turn placing a marble
in the center of the pit. Then each boy shot
a marble into the middle. The rules were
complicated, but the boys knew if they hit
the center marble they got points for the
team, and if they hit the other marbles
they got marbles for themselves.

At first Glass Eyes's team had the lead.
Bobby held onto his cat's eyes. From the

look of the game so far, there was a good chance he would lose his special marbles if he played them. He didn't mind losing a few yellow or red or green marbles, but he didn't have any cat's eyes that he was willing to lose right then.

Pretty soon Glass Eyes got confident with his team's lead. He shot his cat's eyes in the hole. Ezra did the same. Bobby was going to have to match their marbles.

"Come on, you guys. You can't play solid colors against our cat's eyes," Ezra said. Ezra was always the first one to complain. He was also the first one to cheat every chance he got. "Come on," he went on. "Don't be so cheap."

Reluctantly Bobby shot a cat's eye in the hole. Flipper did the same and Speedy followed. Flipper and Speedy lost theirs right away and dropped out of the game. Joey didn't have any cat's eyes to lose, so he stayed in the game for a while, hoping to win some cat's eyes from Glass Eyes.

But Joey kept losing his marbles. "That's it for me," he said finally.

Soupy and Dodgey got tired of the game after a while, even though they were winning, and took off to join the other boys down at the beach.

After a few more minutes, Ezra said, "Okay, I'm out of here. I want to quit while I'm ahead." He followed the other boys.

That left Bobby and Glass Eyes and Lucky, until Bobby told Lucky that he had had all the turns he was going to get and he ran down to the beach after the others.

"That leaves you and me," Bobby said to his cousin.

"What else is new?" Glass Eyes said.

Bobby bent close to the hole to concentrate. He had won two new cat's eyes, but he stood to lose all five if Glass Eyes beat him. One roll after the other. Bobby matched and won, first the solid colored marbles and then, one by one, the cat's eyes until he had all his marbles back plus three extra cat's eyes.

"Okay," Glass Eyes said. "It's time to quit. I'm gonna quit before I lose all my favorite marbles."

"Good idea," Bobby said. He didn't like to see anyone lose, but he loved winning. He concentrated hard on the best way to win each marble until there wasn't one left in the hole. He wasn't the sort of guy to give up and he wasn't the sort of guy to lose. Sometimes when he played on a team and he got close to losing all his marbles, he played extra hard at the end to catch up. And he usually did it. Which was why Bobby was the reserve champion.

He scooped the marbles into the bag. He never stopped to count the cat's eyes. He could tell Glass Eyes wasn't too happy about losing them.

"Come on," Bobby said. "It's hot out here."

"No kidding."

The two boys collapsed under an apple tree on the tall grass. They looked up at the filtered sun sinking low in the sky.

"What time do you think it is?" Bobby asked Glass Eyes.

"I don't know. You got a watch?"

"No. I was thinking of how to tell time without a watch."

"By looking at the sun?"

"Yeah."

Bobby looked across. The sun was sitting in the sky halfway from the mountains to straight up. He remembered his grand-pa telling him that when the sun was right over your head so there was no shadow at all, that meant that it was lunchtime. That's when he and Grandpa went to the house and sat down for fried bread and jam left over from breakfast. Sometimes they would eat fish or clams from the night before.

8

After Bobby won most of the cat's eye marbles that day, the rest of the boys didn't want to play marbles so often. Bobby guessed that they didn't think they would be able to win them back. Bobby missed playing marbles, and he sort of wished he hadn't won so many in the last game. Even Glass Eyes wanted to climb trees or play Monopoly instead.

For the next ten days Bobby spent more time down at Dan's dock. Even when it wasn't Friday night or Saturday, Bobby ran down the path, past the stores and onto the dock. Sometimes he swept up or helped Dan haul in the new boxes of tackle or clean the boats or check gear, but mostly he sprawled on the end of the dock watching his fishing line.

Dan gave Bobby a hook and a bright orange lure that looked like a tiny octopus. Dan said the fish would love it. Bobby went home and found some line in his dad's fishing tackle box. He got a small lead weight, tied it to the end of the line and carefully attached the lure. He dropped the line in the water and watched the bullheads swarm around the hook. He could see they were interested, but they didn't very often bite. Only about once a day would Bobby actually catch one and pull it in. Sometimes he would see a salmon swim by.

One day Bobby lay out lazily on the end of the dock. There weren't many salmon that he could see, so he wrapped the fishing line around his arm, threaded it through his fingers and dozed off. Suddenly he was woken up by a sharp tug on his line. He didn't see anything, but the fish yanked so hard that the line almost cut right through Bobby's finger.

Bobby shook the sleep out of his head and grabbed the line with both hands. He held on tight while the fish swam around until he thought the hook was set firmly in its mouth. Then he started to pull the line up bit by bit.

He made sure he didn't get too excited and try to yank it all up at once. Grandpa had told him that when you get too impatient, the fish will just let go.

"You have to play it," Grandpa used to say. "Sometimes you have to play it until the fish is so tired he just lets you pull him up. It's a contest to see who gets tired first. You or the fish."

Bobby was patient. He played the fish until he could feel it pulling less and less.

"Okay, buddy," Bobby said out loud to the fish. "I win. I'm not even tired and you have given up."

Bobby dragged on the line and wrapped it in a ball in his hand. It was easy at first, but then the fish yanked again and Bobby had to stand up and tighten his fists. He released a little line and waited again until

55

the fish tired out. Bobby let the line out and dragged it in five or six times before the fish finally gave up. Once the line was firm but easy to hold, and it stayed that way for a few minutes, Bobby pulled the line up until he could see the salmon swimming smoothly next to the dock. Then, with a quick motion, Bobby lifted the fish up and laid it at his feet.

The salmon flapped its wet body back and forth. Its silver scales shone in the sun. The fish almost bounced right off the side of the dock before Bobby found a bat.

"Don't think you're getting back in that water," Bobby said. He held the salmon firmly behind the gills, and with one quick smack the fish lay still.

Bobby sized it up. The salmon was as long as from the end of his fingers to his elbow. And it was fat too. It was big enough for Mom to cook for supper.

It was getting late in the afternoon when Bobby wrapped up his fishing gear and tucked it into his pocket. He hooked the salmon on his finger and walked proudly up the dock toward the cleaning counter.

"Hey, son," a man's voice came from the tackle shop. "What do you have there?"

Bobby recognized the voice. It was Uncle Howard.

"Let me look at that," Uncle Howard called down the dock with his booming voice. Dan followed Uncle Howard toward Bobby. "What did you use to get that fine-looking salmon?"

"I used an orange hoochie that Dan gave me and this weight," Bobby said as he pulled the weight out of his pocket. He knew it was important to tell how deep your line was sunk. "This one was a fighter. He wouldn't let me pull him in for nothing."

Bobby slit the belly open to clean the fish and a pocket of small round pink eggs emptied out on the counter.

"Looks like he's a she," Uncle Howard said. "She was a good fighter, you say?"

"That's for sure." Bobby described the pulling in and letting go. He told them about how tired she got and then how hard she yanked and how he had to stand up to keep from letting go. Uncle Howard and Dan listened to every detail.

"This nephew of mine is a real fisherman, Dan," Uncle Howard said as he slapped Bobby on his back. His hand was so big it felt as if he loosened Bobby's teeth. "He takes after me and his old man. It runs in the family from way back. Never no one in our family ever go hungry as long as us fishermen can get out on the water."

Bobby finished cleaning the fish while Uncle Howard and Dan talked about the day's catch. One thing Bobby had learned from being on the dock was that when two men got together, especially when one of them was Dan and the other was Uncle Howard, they could talk about fishing forever.

"It's been good the last few days," Dan said. "They're hauling in cohos and even some good-sized sockeye. It's keeping everyone happy."

"What about this derby you got advertised?"

Uncle Howard pointed to the yellow posters. "Got many kids signed up yet?"

"Thirty so far," Dan said. "Looks like everyone is getting excited. Ten more days yet, so there will probably be forty boats heading out. Our boats will be busy, that's for sure."

"What about you, Bobby?" Uncle Howard said. "You going in the derby?"

"No," Bobby said. He tried not to sound too disappointed. "I'm working on the dock and helping weigh the fish when they come in." Bobby couldn't believe how excited he sounded when he really wasn't excited at all.

"Good for you," Uncle Howard said. "Dan will need a lot of help that day."

"Yeah." Bobby held his head down as he washed the fish blood and guts off the counter. He pulled up the scrub brush and made sure he did a really good job. Not one speck of blood was left. He even scrubbed off the clumps of blood and guts that had dried and stuck like glue from before. He concentrated hard so that Uncle Howard wouldn't see how badly he felt about not signing up for the derby.

It was too late anyway. He had given Mom all the money he had earned both Saturdays since the poster went up. After all, there wasn't a chance that he was going to fish in the derby, and Mom had needed the money badly. It was only a few weeks before all the kids had to go back to school, so there was a lot of things she needed to buy.

9

The Saturday before the derby was different from before. All twenty-one boats were rented, so Bobby was run off his feet packing fishing gear and everything else down to the boats. Some of the fishermen needed help starting their engines, so Bobby gave them a crank or two until the *putt putt putt* began. Usually it was really quiet when the boats were all gone, but this morning people started strolling down to the dock. They milled around this way and that way until they found the bike strung up in the tackle shop. Then they signed up and paid their five dollars.

Bobby was alone in the tackle shop when the woman and the girl walked in.

"Can I help you?" he said.

The little girl could just see over the counter. She was even shorter than Bobby, and he was short for ten. She had long hair about the color of dry grass, only it shone in the sun. It was tied up on each side with red ribbons. At first Bobby thought that the woman and girl were waiting for some fishermen to return or maybe signing up the girl's brother.

"Are you keeping the shop?" the woman asked.

"I can get Dan for you if you want something." Bobby thought the little girl looked just like her mother, who had the reddest lips he had ever seen and the shiniest ones too. "Are you waiting for someone?"

"No," the woman said. "Is this where we sign up for the derby?"

"Yeah," Bobby said.

The little girl yanked on her mother's hand and smiled a very big smile.

"Oh goody, Mom."

Could it be the little girl who was going fishing? Bobby couldn't imagine.

"Do you have any boats to rent?" the mother said.

"I'm not sure. I think they're all rented out."

"Oh dear. We need a boat."

"Aren't we going to be able to enter?" the little girl said. She scrunched her face up, and Bobby was afraid she was going to cry. How was this little girl going to throw in the line or set a lure, never mind pull in a fish? If she did catch a fish, who would club it to death and yank the line out of its mouth?

"Just wait and see, dear." The woman stroked the little girl's long hair.

Bobby lugged the big black book out from under the counter. He opened it up and dragged his finger down the column that said which boats were rented out. It looked to him as if every boat was already booked, but he didn't want to be the one to tell them.

"I better go get Dan for you," Bobby said.

He ran out the door and looked up and down the dock. "Dan," he called. He did not want to go back into the tackle shop alone. "Dan," he shouted.

Finally Dan peered out from behind his boat. He pulled his sanding mask away from his face and laughed his usual laugh. "What's up?" he asked.

Bobby was out of breath and confused as he tried to explain to Dan that someone needed him in the tackle shop. "And it's a girl," Bobby finished. "Her mom wants to sign her up for the derby."

Dan put down his sandpaper and walked up the dock with Bobby.

"A girl, you say?" Dan laughed again. "She wants to enter the derby? Well, she's the first one so far, Bobby. But it wouldn't be the first time a girl went fishing, you know."

Bobby knew that. He had seen women fishing, but usually they were with their husbands. And he had seen girls out with their fathers. But he had never seen just a girl and her mother fishing—especially such a little girl with red ribbons in her hair. There was something about this girl and her mother that didn't bring fishing to mind.

"Good morning," Dan said with a hearty chuckle when he saw the woman and her daughter in the tackle shop. "Can I help you?"

"We want to sign up for the derby," the woman said. "But we need to rent a boat."

"Let's see what we can do for you." Dan looked down at the book. He scanned down the list and up. He counted the names twice.

"Looks to me like we're all booked up," Dan said.

"Oh no," the woman said. Her face twisted up just like her little girl's had. "Angela usually goes fishing with her father, but he's out of town working. He's been gone a very long time, and I promised her that I would enter her in the derby, but I haven't had time to sign her up." The woman's voice was gentle and soft, but Bobby could tell she meant to get what she wanted.

"It's not too late, is it, Mommy?" Bobby thought for sure that the little girl was going to burst into tears. "I'm going to get to go fishing, aren't I?"

Bobby could tell Dan didn't want to see the little girl cry any more than he did. Dan looked back down at the book. Then he looked at the woman.

"You know how to fish?" he asked with a lighthearted laugh.

"Well, not as well as Darren," the woman said seriously. "But Angela and I will do fine. We've been fishing before, haven't we, dear?"

"I want to go fishing," Angela said. "Daddy would take me fishing if he was here."

The lady stroked the little girl's hair again and nodded. Bobby had never seen a kid find a way to get what she wanted like this little girl. She didn't stamp her feet or shout. She didn't even cry. All she did was look like she might.

"Let's put it this way," Dan said. "If these two ladies want to enter the derby, then these two men will sign them up and find them a boat."

When the little girl heard what Dan said, her face opened into a big smile. She tugged so hard on her mom's arm that it looked like she might unhook her shoulder.

"Does that mean we're going to enter the derby, Mommy? Does it?"

"Yes, dear. Now let me get the man the money."

The whole thing surprised Bobby. He still couldn't imagine the woman and her daughter fishing. The more he watched them, the less they looked like fishermen. And how was Dan going to get another boat for them?

Bobby stood next to Dan as the girl and her mother walked up the dock. The little girl wore a fluffy pink dress, white socks and the shiniest black shoes Bobby had ever seen. Her mother stepped carefully over the planks on the dock, making sure the heels on her shoes didn't get stuck in the spaces.

"Who'd figure that, Bobby?" Dan said. "They're the oddest-looking fishermen I've ever seen. Now what we have to do before next Saturday is fix up old Number 1. She hasn't been out for years. I'll fire up the engine. Your job'll be to rub her down and get rid of as much of the chipped paint as you can."

Bobby hadn't thought of Number 1. Dan had said it was the first boat he ever owned. It was retired to the end of the dock where it sat tied up and in the way. But it stayed afloat.

By Sunday, Dan had the engine all fired up and running smoothly. Bobby had cushions on the seats, a fish box under the seat, a club and a net tucked along the side and the old paint scraped off well enough that Number 1 looked like it was ready to go.

"Almost as good as new," Dan said. "She runs like a charm. See you next week, boy. We're going to have a lot of work to do."

Bobby headed up the dock twoard home. He was proud that Dan depended on him to do a good job. He was proud to bring one dollar home to Mom. But when he neared the tackle shop he slowed down and glanced inside at the blue bike. He almost stepped in the door to take a better look, but then he turned away. What was the point of looking at the bike again? By next week some kid would be riding it up and down his street while all the other kids on the street wished it was theirs. Bobby didn't feel proud anymore. He wished he didn't even know about the bike or the derby or Dan Adams.

10

On the morning of the derby, Bobby got up extra early. In fact, he barely slept all night. It was pitch-black outside when he first heard Dan's feet *clunk, clunk, clunk* down the dock. Bobby ate the other half of his peanut butter-and-jam sandwich and gulped down his milk.

The summer was almost over. The morning was chilly and he could smell autumn in the air—blackberries ripening on the vines and oak leaves turning brown. Bobby's feet were cold even though he had worn two pairs of socks to bed and covered his legs with his jacket. He rubbed his feet together and took off his extra pair of socks before he slipped his feet into his shoes. Then he zipped his jacket up to his chin and climbed out of the cabin and down the ladder to the dock.

His eyes took a few minutes to get used to the dark as he stumbled around the side of the boat toward the tackle shop. The light was on and Dan was standing behind the counter.

"Good morning," Bobby called.

"Morning, Bobby," Dan replied. "You're early this morning." Dan was putting tackle from the cardboard boxes into the display case under the counter. "We'd better be ready. Lots of people will need tackle. And they'll need to be taken to their boats."

Dan was excited. Bobby could tell from the sound of his voice and from the planning he was doing and the getting ready, the making sure everything was just right.

"I won a derby when I was a kid," Dan said. He got an extra big smile on his face and he laughed louder than usual. "And you know what I won?"

"No," Bobby answered. "What did you win?"

"You just guess." Dan laughed again.

Bobby couldn't guess. He couldn't think of Dan being a little boy or what he would have won all the way back then.

"Can't guess?" Dan said.

"No."

"I won a blue bike." Dan threw his head back and roared a belly roar. His eyes filled with tears from laughing so much. He stopped laughing and got an excited and serious look on his face as if he were remembering just how he felt. "A braaaandy new blue bike."

That's when Bobby knew why Dan was really excited about the derby.

"And now some other kid is going to win a brand-new blue bike." Dan finished setting the tackle on the shelf. "I can't wait to see the kid's face. It's the most exciting thing in the world. Winning a new bike."

Bobby thought for a moment about just how exciting it would be. And then he closed off that part of his mind. He was one kid who wasn't going to win that blue bike and that was for sure. He didn't even have a chance at it.

"Let's take the bike down from the ceiling and set it up so the kids can see it when they arrive this morning," Dan said.

He reached up and lifted the bike off the hooks.

"Here," he said to Bobby once he got it down. "Push this outside, and we'll figure out some place to display it."

Bobby placed his hands on the rubber handgrips. He held the bike up beside him. He was right. It was a little bit too big. But it wouldn't be long before he would grow and the bike would be just the right size. He stroked his hand across the chrome handlebar. It was so smooth he got shivers up his arms. Then he grabbed the handgrips again and maneuvered the bike out of the small tackle shop. The bike felt just right once Bobby got outside. He imagined throwing his leg over the bar and hitching his butt up onto the seat and riding away.

"Over here," Dan called out. "Let's set it up right here by the cleaning counter. That way all the kids will see it as they head down to their boats."

Bobby followed Dan to the spot and held onto the bike until Dan took it and flipped out the kickstand and stood it next to the tap. The black sky had turned thick gray, just light enough to see. Bobby and Dan stood and looked the bike over.

"Perfect," Dan said. "Don't you think?"

"Yeah," Bobby replied. "Perfect."

Dan set up the second prize next to the bike. It was a bright orange tackle box. Dan opened it up and laid the tackle out so the kids could see the lures and weights and line. He stood a long fishing rod against the pole next to the tackle box. Second prize looked awfully good to Bobby too.

"That's a nice prize," he said to Dan.

"You like that, do you?"

"I've never had a new fishing rod," Bobby said, imagining how he would play a fish on a real fishing rod. "Or a new bike."

Dan didn't hear Bobby because he had already headed up the dock to meet the first fishermen. Bobby followed him a ways behind.

"Good morning," Dan called out to a man and his sons. "It's a great morning for fishing. I hear the fish chomping right now. They're ready to bite." Dan chuckled.

"We sure hope so," the man said.

"And I'm going to catch the biggest one of all," the youngest boy added.

"No, I am," the other boy said. "Aren't I, Dad?"

"While you guys decide who's catching the biggest fish," the man said, "I have to get a few lures."

Dan turned to Bobby. "I'll take care of the shop," he said. "You take the people down to their boats. I'll let you know which boat they've reserved."

Bobby was ready. The morning was going to be busy. Everyone was going to arrive at once.

When the boys came out of the shop with their father, Bobby led them down to their boat and showed them the life jackets and fish box. He plopped their gear down.

"Have a good time," Bobby said as they pulled the crank and started the engine. "Hope you catch the biggest fish."

"I'm gonna," both boys said at once.

All three waved at Bobby.

11

The fishermen arrived quickly, one group after the other. Bobby barely had one group settled in their boat before another wandered down the dock. Fathers came with their sons, grandfathers with their grandsons and even a few uncles with their nephews.

"Have a good time," Bobby called to the group in Number 3, *Shrimp*. "Hope you catch a big fish." I wouldn't want my boat to be called *Shrimp*, Bobby thought, not if I was in a fishing derby and hoping to catch the biggest fish of all. Better to be in Number 11, *Kingfisher*, or Number 12, *Tuna*. Tuna were the biggest fish of all.

When Bobby headed back up the dock to meet the next fishermen, he heard a boy shout, "I don't want to carry the tackle box. There's the kid right there. Get him to do it."

Two men and a boy were coming toward Bobby. The boy was just a little taller than he was but a whole lot skinnier. When he saw Bobby he dropped the tackle box onto the dock and stamped one foot against the other and swung his arms until they were wrapped tightly around his chest.

"It's too heavy," he screamed. "Let him carry it. He works here."

"You pick that up and carry it to the boat, Patrick." The father spoke much more quietly than the son. "Please."

"I'm not going fishing if I have to carry that thing all the way down to the boat." The boy plunked his bottom right down on the dock next to his tackle box.

"Please, Patrick," the father said. "We have to find our boat."

"No way. It's too heavy." The boy's voice sounded like he hurt really bad, but Bobby couldn't see what his problem was.

Bobby wasn't sure what to do. Should he pick up the tackle box and carry it for the boy? Should he leave the family to fight it out? Or should he stand and wait to help them?

"You take it," Patrick shouted at Bobby.

Bobby looked past the boy. "Would you like me to show you to your boat?" he said to the father.

The man slouched his shoulders, reached down and picked up the tackle box.

"Yes," he said. "Come on, then, Patrick. It's getting late. We want to get out on the water as soon as we can."

The second the father picked up the tackle box, the boy jumped up and headed down the dock.

"We'll win first prize, won't we, Dad?" he said as if he had forgotten all about sitting on the dock and shouting. "I'm gonna get that bike."

Bobby brought them down to Number 8, *Abalone*, and showed them where the gear was stored.

"It's cold, Dad," the boy whined. "I want another jacket. Can I wear your jacket, Uncle Sam?"

The other man looked impatient with the boy. "No, Patrick," he said. "Wrap yourself in the blanket."

"Uncle Sam, I'm cold. I can't wrap myself in a blanket. How can I fish if I'm wrapped in a blanket?" The boy's voice got louder and higher each time he said something. "And I'm hungry. What did we bring to eat?"

Bobby didn't know how the boy was going to be able to fish anyway. He never sat still long enough for a fish to bite. And he wasn't quiet long enough to figure out where the fish were biting or where the seagulls were feeding or how the tide was running.

"Dad! Dad!"

"Now what do you want?" the father said.

"I have to go to the bathroom," the boy whimpered. "In a hurry."

"Come on, Patrick," the uncle said. "We want to get out of here and do some fishing."

"Follow me," Bobby said. "There's an out-house down by the beach."

The boy huffed and puffed and scuffled his feet and smacked his lips all the way to the outhouse.

"Wait for me," he said to Bobby. "I don't know my way back."

Bobby was sure of one thing while he waited outside the small wooden shed. Patrick probably had a new bike at home. If he didn't he would get one if he whined enough. And Bobby knew one more thing. He didn't want Patrick to win. It would spoil the whole derby if a kid who whined and cried as much as Patrick won the new blue bike.

Once Patrick came out he ran ahead of Bobby to the boat.

"Have a good time," Bobby called out as they putted away. He didn't say, "And I hope you catch a big fish." He didn't really hope that at all. Not for that boat.

Bobby counted the boats still tied up to the dock. Four. Old Number 1 was still tied to the end, getting in the way. It was almost light out except for a slight gray tinge to the sky. When Bobby got back to the tackle shop, no one was there except Dan, restocking the counter.

"Almost got everyone?" Dan said.

"Only four boats to go," Bobby replied.

"Been a great morning," Dan said. "Everyone's excited and ready to have a good time."

Soon Bobby heard a woman's voice outside.

"Good morning," Dan said when the little girl and her mother entered the shop. "You two ready to fish?"

"We sure are," the woman said.

"Yeah," the little girl said. "We're going to catch a big fish, aren't we, Mommy?"

They each carried a fishing rod and tackle box and had backpacks strapped over their shoulders. The little girl wore a baseball cap, boots and a big heavy coat. Her mother was dressed the same way. They looked nothing like they had the week before when they had signed up for the derby. "I'll take them down to their boat,

Bobby," Dan said with a good-natured laugh. "You take care of the shop."

Bobby watched Dan lead the woman and her daughter down the dock. But instead of going to old Number 1, he stopped in front of Number 10 *Coho*. He started the engine up and waved to them as they putted out into the bay.

When Dan got back to the tackle shop, he looked at Bobby's confused face.

"Only ladies we got. I thought we should take care of them," Dan said with a laugh.

12

Soon the other three groups of fishermen came and went. When the last boat took off into the bay, Dan and Bobby slumped in the chairs outside the tackle shop. They were quiet for a few moments, breathing deeply to catch their breath. In the quiet Bobby heard a gentle *plip plip plip*. He looked around to see where the noise was coming from.

Plip plip plip. It was the sound of a paddle dipping into the water, but he couldn't see a canoe anywhere.

Suddenly, from behind the tackle shop, he heard a booming voice.

"Hey, nephew, hurry up. Don't just sit there. We got fishing to do." Uncle Howard pulled the canoe against the dock.

"I didn't think you were gonna make it," Dan said. "Hurry up, Bobby. You gotta get back here before the fishermen get in."

Bobby looked at Uncle Howard and then he looked at Dan. He looked at Dan and then back at Uncle Howard. Both men laughed. Bobby could tell they knew something he didn't.

"Come on, nephew," Uncle Howard shouted. "You want to fish or not?"

"Me?" Bobby said. "Do I want to fish?"

"That's what I said, didn't I? The canoe is all fired up and the engine's ready to go." Uncle Howard flexed his arms.

Bobby looked back at Dan.

"He's right, Bobby. Howard paid me the five bucks and said he'd pick you up when the work was done and get you back before the work started again," Dan said. "So hurry up. If you're going to catch the biggest fish, you better get off your haunches and get started."

Bobby sprang out of his chair. Had a dream got started right there in the middle of the morning when he was wide-awake? He wanted to pinch himself to make sure it was real, but Uncle Howard looked real enough. Bobby felt real enough too when Dan slapped him on the back as they headed toward Uncle Howard's canoe.

"We'll see you around ten-thirty," Uncle Howard said to Dan.

"That's great," Dan said. "Don't be late. I need Bobby's help."

"I'll give you a hand later if you want," Uncle Howard called out.

"Thanks. Good luck, Bobby. Catch the big one!" Dan waved his hand and laughed all the way back to the tackle shop.

Bobby stepped into the canoe, picked up his paddle and dipped it in the water.

"You get the line ready, Bobby. This is your fishing trip. I'll paddle," Uncle Howard said.

That was different. Usually when they went fishing, Bobby had to paddle most of the time and Uncle Howard held the lines, baited up and pulled the fish in. He only let Bobby cast his own line once in a while. So Bobby got really good at paddling and at watching his uncle fish. He knew just what to do.

Bobby dipped his hands into the water and rubbed his fingers together. To get the smell of humans off his hands, Grandpa had told him. Fish can smell people a mile away.

He tied the lure onto the line and dragged the hook over his finger to make sure it was sharp. He looped the line in a perfect knot around the round stone Uncle Howard had covered with nylon stockings on the line.

The canoe glided silently through the glassy water. Not a breath of wind disturbed the bay. Only the *putt putt putt* of the fish boats and the *plip plip plip* of the canoe paddle broke the silence. Most of the boats had their lines out and were putting around in circles, waiting for the fish to bite.

"We're heading over to Indian Bay," Uncle Howard said. "I'd go down to McKenzie Bight, but we don't have time to get there and back before ten-thirty. I figure we'll stay close to home."

Indian Bay was right in front of Bobby's house and just around the point from the marina.

"Cast that line any time now, Bobby. I checked it out on my way over and I figure the seagulls are telling me this is a good spot. The tides are telling me the same thing, and when I asked the Creator this morning, he agreed."

Bobby threw the line into the water. He felt the weight sink until there was a steady tug on the line.

"But when I asked Elmer he said Indian Bay would be dry this morning and that he was headed over to Bamberton. It looks like a lot of fishermen are over there with him." Uncle Howard squinted across the bay to Bamberton.

Bobby watched the rhythm of his line against the inky black water.

"Let's hope Elmer's wrong," he said.

Uncle Howard lifted his arms and dipped the paddle into the water in long powerful strokes. The canoe traveled through the water as quickly as the boats that were trolling alongside. Most of the boats had headed across to Bamberton as Uncle Howard said, but a few were trolling around Indian Bay.

Low early morning rays shone across the water and washed the gray sky with streaks of bright blue-green, apricot and lavender.

"You're gonna catch a big one," Uncle Howard said. "I can feel it in my bones."

Bobby couldn't feel it in his bones. But something was working on his side this morning. He could hardly believe he was fishing, yet he was. It was better than a dream. So he let himself believe for a few moments that it was also possible he would catch the biggest fish.

"How will you know when it's ten-thirty and we have to go in?" Bobby asked. He had never seen a watch on Uncle Howard's wrist. He had never seen a clock in his house either, for that matter.

"I watch the sun." Uncle Howard pointed with his chin toward the sun. "When it's there," he dipped his head to the side and lifted his chin low in the sky toward Dan's marina, "it's about nine o'clock. When the sun is there," he pointed his chin higher above his head, bending it slightly to the left, "it's about ten o'clock. And when the sun is about there," he pointed again a little higher than the last time, "it's gonna be about ten-thirty and we better be pulling up beside Dan's dock and hauling the biggest fish of the derby up to the cleaning counter to be weighed."

Bobby watched the end of the line nodding in a steady rhythm toward the water. Suddenly the rhythm was interrupted. The rod jerked so hard Bobby almost lost his grip on the handle.

"You got one," Uncle Howard said. "Pull her in."

Bobby's heart jumped when he felt the pressure. He knew it was a big one.

He balanced his knees against the side of the canoe. Just when he reached down to loosen the line, the end of the rod dipped limply in the water. Bobby gave the rod a tug, but instead of feeling a fish he felt the familiar nodding rhythm of an empty line.

"Looks like she got away on you," Uncle Howard said. "And she was a big one."

The big one got away. Bobby didn't like how that sounded.

His hands trembled as he pulled in the line to check. Sure enough, the fish had eaten his bait and taken the hook with it.

"Don't worry, son," Uncle Howard said. "Now we know we're in the right spot."

Uncle Howard sounded a lot more confident than Bobby felt. When Bobby watched the end of his line, all he could think about was the blue bike. That fish took the bait and Bobby's chance at winning the derby. He knew as he watched the sun moving higher in the sky that he barely had any time for another fish to bite.

Just when Uncle Howard said, "Look over there!" and Bobby caught a glimpse of an eagle circling low overhead, he felt a second heavy tug on the line. The end of the fishing rod bent until it touched the water. It wasn't a quick jerk like the last time, or the tug where the line pulls back and then forward. This was just one long tug bending the rod lower and lower.

"Have I caught the bottom?" Bobby asked.

"Let out some line," Uncle Howard said. "Loosen your reel."

When Bobby loosened the clip, his reel spun out of control.

"Shut her down," Uncle Howard shouted. "I think you got one."

Bobby held onto the rod with both hands. It was heavy and hard to hold onto as his rod bent again into the water.

"It's not the bottom, son. It's a mighty big fish," Uncle Howard announced.

Bobby held onto the rod and let the fish play the hook. He felt it move at the other end of his fishing line. The fish dodged from side to side, pulling the line back and forth.

"Let him go, Bobby. He has to get the hook set in his mouth. He's playing you, trying to get himself free."

94

Uncle Howard kept paddling the canoe steady and strong. They traveled in a long oval right in front of the reserve. If Bobby had looked up he would have seen his mom standing on their front porch, waving at him. Uncle Howard had told her of his plan. She was calling out, "I hope you get a big fish," but Bobby couldn't hear her.

Bobby pulled the rod in and then let it out. When the tip of the line bent to the water, Uncle Howard told Bobby to let out some more line. He loosened the clip and the reel spun until Bobby tightened it up again.

"How much line should I let out?" Bobby asked.

"As much as you need to keep the big one on the hook," Uncle Howard said. "You gotta play this one till he gets tired, son. Are you all right?"

"I'm fine," Bobby said. "I'll play him until I pull him into the canoe."

But Bobby's arms and shoulders were getting pretty tired. He had a pain in his back from trying to keep the rod up and steady and trying not to let go of it when the reel was spinning out of control.

Finally it felt as if the fish had stopped fighting. It would be a long job pulling it in. Slowly and steadily Bobby reeled the line up. If he felt the fish tug hard, he let it out again. Then he turned the reel again to bring the fish closer to the boat.

Bobby watched the sun move high over his shoulder. It was getting late. The fish was taking most of the morning to get caught. Bobby could tell that it was time to head back to the marina because he was getting tired and hungry. But he didn't stop for a moment. If he did he could lose the fish altogether.

13

Bobby's arms were numb and his fingers were white by the time he saw the giant salmon swimming from side to side of the canoe. He wasn't absolutely sure it was a spring, but its nose was dark and it wasn't fighting as much as a coho would. The silver scales glistened like tinfoil under the midmorning sun. It was the biggest fish Bobby had ever pulled in and it might be the biggest fish he had ever seen swimming like that in the water around the canoe. Bobby's whole body felt like jelly. Every bit of strength he had was gone. He wondered if his shoulders and arms and hands and fingers could hold on for another second.

"That was the easy part," Uncle Howard said. "The tough part is getting him into the net without knocking him off the hook, and hauling him into the boat without tipping yourself into the water."

What Uncle Howard said was true. Bobby had to hold onto the rod with one hand and scoop the net into the water with the other hand, and he had to do it at the right moment when the fish was beside the canoe. He had to capture the fish head-first without knocking the hook out of his mouth.

Bobby stuck the fishing pole between his legs and lodged it against the bottom of the canoe. He held it steady with one arm while Uncle Howard passed him the net.

"It's up to you, nephew." Uncle Howard's voice was as steady as his strokes. "Let him swim right into your net. Then you'll have him."

Bobby was quiet and careful. He watched the fish glide through the water. He wanted to dip the net into the water right away and capture the fish, but he decided to wait and watch. He watched the fish swim back and forth until he knew just where to dip his net into the water. He watched the fish's pattern a few more times. The fish swam slowly over and over in the same circle.

Slowly Bobby lifted the net over the side of the canoe, making sure he held firm to the pole. He placed the net into the water just in front of the fish, and the fish swam right into the net. Once the fish was all the way in, Bobby let go of his pole and placed both hands on the net's handle. When the fish came up against the net, he flapped his body back and forth, pulling Bobby to one side and then the other. The canoe rocked and Bobby banged his elbows against the cedar. He braced his feet firmly on the floor of the canoe to keep from teetering into the water.

"Keep him in the water until you have full control, Bobby. Get a firm grip on the handle up close to the net."

Bobby did exactly what Uncle Howard said. He gripped the handle so close to the net that the fish's tail slapped his white knuckles. Then he stood up and with a single scoop lifted the net, fish and all, into the canoe.

The net was a tangled mess, but the fish was trapped. Bobby picked up the club. He tried to hold the fish's head steady as he hit it, but each time Bobby hit the fish it seemed to flap more furiously than before. Finally it lay still on the bottom of the canoe, splattered with blood and tangled in the net.

Only then did Bobby feel the pain in his arms and his shoulders and fingers.

"That is one beautiful salmon," Uncle Howard said. "Looks like a winner to me."

Bobby had forgotten about winning. He had forgotten about everything except pulling the fish safely into the canoe. He had forgotten about the time as well.

"We better hustle back," Uncle Howard said. "Dan will be waiting."

Bobby was too tired to help Uncle Howard paddle back to the marina. His arms felt like jelly and his fingers felt like nothing at all except maybe rubber. Bobby just sat in a heap in the front of the canoe and rubbed his arms and shoulders.

"Hurry up," Dan yelled across the water. He waved his arms to the canoe. "It's ten-thirty and we've got work to do."

When the canoe bumped gently against the dock, Dan held out his hand to pull Bobby up. It felt like Bobby's arm was going to split off at the shoulder. When he was out of the canoe, Dan looked down and saw the fish still wrapped in the net.

Dan's eyes lit up and he smiled as big as he could smile. "Look at that!" He broke into loud laughter. "Will you look at that!"

"It's a big one," Uncle Howard said. "You should have seen my nephew play it. That fish meant to make a fisherman out of him. He was willing to give up his life for Bobby, but not without a fight."

"You got a winner there, Bobby," Dan said. He was still laughing.

"He netted it like an old pro," Uncle Howard continued. "Waited for the perfect moment, studied the fish until he knew exactly when to dip that net. The poor old fish swam right into it. And that was the end of it."

As Uncle Howard was talking, Dan pulled the fish and the net out of the boat. He untangled the line and pulled the hook out of the fish's mouth. He curled his fingers under the salmon and held the fish up in the air. He lifted it and dropped it down as if it was hanging on a scale.

"What do you say, Howard?" Dan's forehead wrinkled into a deep V. "About fourteen, maybe sixteen pounds?"

"Looks at least that big to me," Uncle Howard replied.

"It felt like it weighed as much as me," Bobby said. He had never seen a fish look more beautiful than that fish as it hung on Dan's finger.

Uncle Howard tied the canoe to the dock and jumped out.

"Let's weigh it and see."

Dan had brought the scales out and hung them above the cleaning counter. He had nailed a giant chalkboard on a post next to the scales. At the top of one column he had written "NAME." Another column said "AGE," and the last column said "FISH WEIGHT." That was the column to watch out for. The kid with the heaviest fish would win the bike. Now that Bobby was back on the dock, he got to thinking about the bike.

It wasn't propped up next to the cleaning counter anymore.

"Where's the bike?" he said to Dan.

"I brought it back into the tackle shop. Keep it out of the way until all the weighing and cleaning is finished."

Dan lifted Bobby's fish and hooked it onto the giant hook attached to the scale. Then he took the small iron blocks and added them one at a time to the scale until the fish and the iron blocks were perfectly balanced. Then he added up how many pounds of iron he had loaded on.

"Sixteen pounds, seven ounces," Dan said. "That's a beauty, Bobby, my boy. That could be a winning fish."

Bobby watched his fish hanging from the scale. He watched Dan write Bobby A. in the first column under "NAME." Dan wrote ten in the second column under "AGE." And then sixteen pounds, seven ounces, in the third column under "WEIGHT." Bobby liked seeing his name on the board. But a hard lump sat in the bottom of his stomach when he thought that maybe, just maybe, he had a chance to win the bike.

14

The first boat didn't pull up to the dock until eleven o'clock. By then Bobby had the feeling back in his arms and hands, and his shoulders didn't hurt as much.

"How did you do?" Bobby called out as the man shut off the engine. He threw Bobby the rope, and Bobby tied the boat securely to the dock. The man and the boy looked tired.

"We did really well," the man said. He looked happy with his catch. "Peter pulled in four fish and I got two, but none of them are going to win any prize for being the biggest. At least I don't think so."

The man lugged the fish box up onto the dock. He was right. They had six good-looking fish, but none of them could have been much bigger than six pounds.

When they got the fish up to the scales, the boy's biggest fish weighed in at seven pounds. Dan wrote Peter J. in the first column, eleven in the second, and seven pounds, five ounces, in the third column.

The man looked at Bobby's fish. Then he looked at Bobby. "That's one fine-looking fish for a small guy like you to pull in," he said. "You've got something to be proud of, young man."

Uncle Howard helped Peter gut his fish. He showed him how to hold the fish without cutting his fingers and how to tell a male fish from a female.

"You want me to show you how to fillet the fish?" Uncle Howard asked.

"What does that mean?" Peter asked him.

"That means you cut the skeleton and bones out so the fish is ready to cook or ready to smoke."

"Sure," Peter said.

Uncle Howard slipped the tip of his sharp knife under the backbone. He slid the knife up both sides so close to the bones that barely any meat was left attached. In a few moments the fish lay on one side of the counter and the clean white bones of the skeleton lay on the other.

"Wow!" Peter said. "Thanks."

"You want to try?" Uncle Howard asked him.

Peter took the knife and copied Uncle Howard. The only difference was there was a big pile of red fish meat stuck to the bones when he was finished. And there was a lot of fish meat on the counter and on Peter's hands and on the front of his shirt.

"Well done," Uncle Howard said. "A little practice and you'll be great."

Peter smiled. He said he didn't like the bones anyway, and this meant his mom could cook it up right away. Maybe even for supper.

Peter smiled again as he packed his fish in a bag and staggered up the dock.

"If your fish is second biggest we'll phone you and let you know," Dan said. "Thanks for joining our derby."

"Thank you," the man said.

"Yeah, thanks," Peter added. "I had lots of fun."

Slowly the small boats returned. When they hit the dock, Bobby ran down to greet them. Each time he peered into the boat first to see the fish box. He was the only fisherman who came in with just one fish. Most of the fish boxes were full or at least half full.

When the little girl came in with her mother, Bobby was waiting for them.

"How did you do?" he shouted. He caught the rope when the woman swung it over to him.

"We did great," the woman said. "Angela pulled in her first fish all by herself. Just like the contest said. The kid had to catch it, pull it in and net it herself. And she did."

When Bobby looked in their fish box, his heart skipped a beat. Only two fish lay on the bottom of the box. One small fish and one big fish. The big fish looked like it was as big as, or maybe even bigger than, his fish, which was hanging on a hook next to the chalkboard. Beside his fish, Dan had written, "The fish to beat, so far. Caught by Bobby Alexander."

"That's a big fish," Bobby stammered.

"Isn't it beautiful?" Angela said. She sounded tired and excited at the same time.

Her mother tossed their blankets and thermoses and backpacks up onto the dock. She heaved the fish box up next to Bobby's foot. He bent down and looked closely at the fish. He squinted his eyes to look up the dock at his fish hanging on display. He looked back at the big fish.

"She did really well. I didn't do a thing," the mother said. Bobby tried to imagine the little girl pulling in such a big fish. "Her father would be so proud of her today. But I was the one who got the biggest fish."

"You?" Bobby stammered. "You pulled in the big one?"

"You bet," the mother said. "And Angela pulled in the small one."

"Isn't it pretty?" Angela said. "Wait till Daddy sees a picture of me and my fish."

Bobby lugged the fish box up the dock to the scale. Dan's mouth gaped when he saw the big fish.

"Looks like we got the prize for the biggest fish caught by a girl in this derby. And the biggest fish caught by a lady," Uncle Howard said. "You got a prize for that, Dan?"

Angela's fish weighed four pounds, two ounces, and her mother's fish weighed eighteen pounds. Bobby was happy that her fish didn't count.

When Angela saw Bobby's name next to the sign that said, "The fish to beat," she said, "Wow, Bobby! You must be a good fisherman. I hope you win the derby."

Angela said to her mother, "Can we wait and see if Bobby wins?" Her mother agreed and together they watched each boat as it returned.

Soon the dock was full of fishermen. Bobby ran from one boat to the next, swallowing the lump in his stomach as he checked out each fish box. Some boxes were full of little fish and others were full of big fish. Some looked as big as Bobby's, but when Dan weighed the fish and filled in the chart on the chalkboard it looked like this:

NAME	AGE	FISH WEIGHT
Bobby A.	10	16 pounds 7 ounces
Peter J.	11	7 pounds 5 ounces
Lester S.	12	14 pounds 6 ounces
Donald L.	11	10 pounds 9 ounces
Richard C.	8	5 pounds 2 ounces
Mark H.	10	9 pounds 11 ounces
Stephen R.	9	7 pounds 4 ounces
Bryon T.	10	13 pounds 8 ounces

Pretty soon there were thirty-six names on the list. When Dan weighed Raymond Blacker's fish, Bobby held his breath.

"It's not as big as your fish, Bobby," Angela said. "I know it's not."

But it wasn't until Dan announced fifteen pounds, one ounce, that Bobby took a deep breath. Other fish came close to being as big as Bobby's, but his fish and his name stayed on the board under the place that said, "The fish to beat, so far."

The closer it got to the one o'clock deadline, the busier it got. Bobby counted the boats. Most of them were already in when he saw Patrick and his father and uncle com-ing toward the dock. From where Bobby stood next to the cleaning counter he could hear Patrick shouting at the top of his lungs. Bobby couldn't tell for sure what he was saying, but it sounded like he was saying something about catching the biggest fish.

Reluctantly Bobby walked down the dock to meet the boat. What if Patrick was right? He sucked back a big mouthful of air to drive the lump in his stomach down deep. He wanted to look at the fish, but he didn't want to look at the fish.

When their boat hit the dock, Patrick sprang onto the dock as if he had wires on his feet.

"I won," he shouted. "I know I won. You gotta look at the fish I got."

Bobby leaned over the dock and peered into the boat. He looked around for the fish box. There were four or five fish lying in the bottom of the box, and spread out on top was the biggest fish Bobby had seen for a long time. There was no getting around it. The fish was bigger than Bobby's. It was longer and it was fatter. It had to weigh more than his fish. It probably weighed a lot more.

"Did Patrick pull in that fish?" Bobby asked no one in particular.

No one answered. When he looked up at the two men, they had grumpy looks on their faces.

"Here, young fellow," the uncle said to Bobby. "Can you help haul our stuff up the dock? I'll pack the fish box."

"I won! I won!" Patrick shouted at the top of his lungs. "I'm gonna get a new bike, aren't I, Daddy?"

His dad didn't say much other than "Settle down, Patrick. Can't you be a little quieter?"

His uncle didn't pay any attention to Patrick at all. As far as Bobby could see, the uncle wished Patrick wasn't even there.

The dock was full of people milling around, looking at Bobby's fish hanging next to the chart, and waiting to see if someone was going to beat it. They had their cameras ready to take a picture of the winner with his fish and his new bike. When Patrick announced that he had the biggest fish, everyone waited anxiously to get a look at it.

The uncle plunked the fish box in front of the cleaning counter. Uncle Howard lifted the enormous fish. His muscles flexed as he hefted it onto the scales. Dan added iron weights until the scale balanced. Then he counted the weights.

"Twenty pounds, three ounces," Dan announced to the crowd.

"What a fish!" someone exclaimed.

"Way to go, boy!" someone else shouted.

Everyone clapped and cheered and pushed forward toward the scale to get a closer look at the fish.

When Bobby realized how much the fish weighed, he swallowed hard. Then he swallowed even harder to stop tears from filling his eyes.

"Do you think that skinny brat could have pulled a huge fish like that into the boat?"

Bobby turned around. Angela stood behind him.

"He says he did."

"I don't think so," she said.

"Neither do I."

Bobby was positive. Angela was right.

"He's no bigger than me," she added.

She was right about that too.

Patrick raced around the dock hollering at the top of his lungs.

"Where's my new bike?"

His dad stood quietly next to his uncle.

"Wait," his dad said. He grabbed Patrick's arm and tried to settle him down. "There are still a few boats to come in."

He looked at his watch. Twenty minutes remained.

"But I won, Dad, didn't I?" Patrick said again and again as he wriggled free from his father's grip.

Dan looked at Patrick. He looked at the fish. He looked at Patrick's dad and uncle.

"This young fellow caught this mighty big fish?" he asked.

The uncle looked away and said nothing. The father just nodded.

"That's my fish," Patrick shouted. "That's the one I caught."

Dan lifted Bobby's fish off the winning hook and replaced it with Patrick's fish. It was a beautiful fish; Bobby had to admit that. He wished he had caught it. He imagined how big it would have looked in the water, swimming around the front of the canoe. But then he thought about pulling it in, and Bobby didn't think he could have done it. Bobby didn't think he could have pulled in a fish one ounce bigger than the one he got. When he looked at Patrick, he knew Patrick didn't pull the great big fish in either.

"Well, Bobby," Dan said quietly. "You have a good second place."

"I couldn't have pulled that great big fish in," Bobby said.

"That skinny kid couldn't have pulled it in either," Angela said.

To Bobby's surprise, at one o'clock, when all the boats were back and the fish were weighed, Glass Eyes and Ezra and Soupy and Flipper and Dodgey showed up on the dock. They looked the big fish on the winning hook up and down. They looked Patrick up and down.

"He the guy who says he caught that fish?" Soupy said in a voice much louder than Angela's.

Dan heard him as he brought the bike out onto the dock and placed the tackle box and fishing rod on the cleaning counter. Everyone else heard him too.

Dan said, "Yeah, he's the winner all right."

He stood next to the winning fish, ready to make the announcement.

Angela moved next to Soupy. "I doubt it, don't you?" she said.

"Can't imagine a skinny little runt like him pulling in a fish like that," Soupy said. "I couldn't pull that one in myself."

Soupy couldn't pull in a fish half that size, Bobby thought. But he didn't want to say a thing. He couldn't say a thing. All he could do was look at the blue bike and wish that his fish was still hanging on the hook and that his name was still printed next to "The fish to beat."

Dan looked troubled when he turned away from Soupy and faced the crowd.

"Well," he said, "it looks like we have a winner. It looks like we have lots of winners, but we only have prizes for two or maybe three."

Dan's forehead creased into a deep V. He shifted from one foot to the other. He didn't look as excited as he had before Patrick had come in with his fish. Dan's eyes moved from Patrick's fish to Bobby and Angela. He didn't look at Soupy.

"Let's go over the rules just to make sure everyone's got them right." Dan pulled an old poster off the pole and read the rules one by one out loud to the crowd.

After he finished reading, he said, "We have a mighty big fish here, and we gotta congratulate the boy who pulled this beauty in. Because he's our winner."

Patrick ran up to the front and leaped in front of Dan.

"You must be some kind of fisherman, young man, to be able to pull in a great big fish like this."

"I won," Patrick shouted. "I got the biggest fish, didn't I, Dad?"

Although Patrick looked happy about winning, his dad didn't look very happy at all. And when Bobby looked at the uncle, he could see Patrick's uncle looked downright angry. Dan wasn't laughing his usual laugh. And Angela looked like she might start crying any minute. All of a sudden the fishing derby wasn't any fun at all.

Angela moved close to Bobby again and tugged on his shirt. "Tell them, Bobby," she said. "Tell them." But something inside

Bobby made him think that everyone had said enough. He kept his eyes on Dan.

Just as Dan was about to present the bike to Patrick, he put his hand on the small boy's shoulder and said firmly, "Are you sure you pulled this fish into the boat, young man?"

Before Patrick had time to answer, his uncle stepped forward.

"Who is Bobby Alexander? The boy who caught the sixteen pound, seven ounce, fish?"

"This is him right here," Dan said. "He's my right-hand man. And a mighty good fisherman as well."

"Well, he's the winner," the uncle said loudly. He pulled Bobby to the front of the crowd. "Bobby Alexander is the winner."

The crowd became very quiet except for Patrick. Patrick screamed at his uncle and broke into tears and loud wet sobs.

"Patrick didn't pull in this fish. His dad did. And I helped out a lot. You see, Patrick wanted to win so badly my brother and I let him think he had won.

But that wasn't the rules, and I like to play by the rules."

It was almost too good to be true.

The dad joined in. "Yes," he said more quietly than the uncle. "Patrick wouldn't have it any other way. I was wrong."

"I won, Dad," Patrick shrieked. "You said I won."

Patrick made such a noise it was hard to hear what his father said. The two men took Patrick to the end of the dock. Bobby didn't hear what they said, but after a few minutes Patrick came back to the crowd with his dad and uncle and never said another word. Bobby thought they probably promised to buy him a new bike anyway.

Dan took the big fish down and set Bobby's back up on the hook. He erased Patrick's name and filled the space in once again with "Bobby Alexander." Then he placed the new blue bike in front of Bobby and announced the winner of the 1957 Dan Adams's fishing derby.

"The winner is Bobby Alexander."

KIDS FISHING DERBY
1957

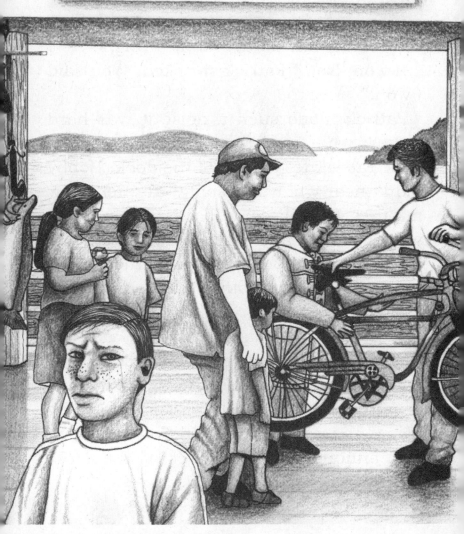

Dan laughed a big laugh, and when Bobby looked up at his face he thought he saw tears in his eyes, although he wasn't sure.

Uncle Howard stood in front of the crowd and thanked Dan for putting on such a good fishing derby.

"And we have a special prize for the biggest fish caught by a girl," Uncle Howard announced. "Dan has offered a free boat rental for Angela Tinney and her mother."

Angela jumped up and yelled, "We both won, Bobby!"

Angela and her mother hugged Dan and Uncle Howard, which made the men smile. After a lot of pictures were taken, Uncle Howard continued.

"I want to take the time to say one more thing. I want to tell all you folks that young Bobby is the best young fisherman I have seen in a long time." Uncle Howard looked proudly at his nephew. "And he takes after his uncle."

Sylvia Olsen never runs out of ideas for her stories. After all, her mother and mother-in-law have more than two hundred grandchildren and great-grand-children between them! Like Bobby, she lives in Tsartlip First Nation, where she has lived for almost thirty years. She works as a First Nations community development consultant. She got the idea for *Catching Spring* from her children's father, who entered a fishing derby when he was a boy. Sylvia is the author of two other novels for children and teens, *No Time to Say Goodbye* and *The Girl With a Baby*.